Second Grade

HOLDOUT

Written by Audrey Vernick • Illustrated by Matthew Cordell

CLARION BOOKS
Houghton Mifflin Harcourt   Boston   New York

For Mrs. Gidaro's class and for Mrs. Hackler
and all my friends at the Wayside School
—A.V.

For my favorite 2nd grader (soon to be favorite 3rd grader), Romy Bess
—M.C.

Clarion Books
3 Park Avenue
New York, New York 10016

Clarion Books is an imprint of Houghton Mifflin Harcourt Publishing Company.

www.hmhco.com

The illustrations in this book were done in pen and ink with watercolor.
The text was set in Amasis MT std.

Library of Congress Cataloging-in-Publication Data
Names: Vernick, Audrey, author. | Cordell, Matthew, 1975- illustrator.
Title: Second grade holdout / written by Audrey Vernick ;
illustrated by Matthew Cordell.
Description: Boston ; New York : Clarion Books, Houghton Mifflin Harcourt,
[2017] | Summary: Missing the familiarity of first grade and
imagining the impossible tasks assigned by his next teacher,
a boy refuses to start second grade.
Identifiers: LCCN 2016010617 | ISBN 9780544876811 (hardcover)
Subjects: | CYAC: Schools—Fiction. | First day of school—Fiction.
Classification: LCC PZ7.V5973 Sec 2017 | DDC [E]—dc23
LC record available at https://lccn.loc.gov/2016010617

Manufactured in China
SCP 10 9 8 7 6 5 4 3 2 1
4500646575

I was a lot of things in first grade.

Trash Collector.

Confused.

Star of the Day.

Unable to sit still
(according to Ms. Morgan).

In the same class as my best friend, Tyler.

Second grade is going to be different.

We probably won't get fun jobs to do every day.

"Your job is to be a good student," Dad says.

That's just one example of why second grade is not for me.

Also, Tyler's going to be in Mrs. Herman's class.

And I'll be in Mr. Glazer's class.

I had the clever idea that I could switch into Mrs. Herman's class with Tyler,

but my parents said that wasn't going to happen.

So I got an even cleverer idea.

Staying in first grade.

I mean, what's so great about second grade?

First grade was pretty awesome.

And Ms. Morgan *gets* me.

If I stick with her in good old room 101, I could be Lakeview Elementary's smartest-ever first-grader! They might have medals and certificates for that. Maybe a crown of some kind.

Mom is not on board with this plan.

"Don't you want to get better at reading? And learn to make graphs?" she asks.

I'm okay with skipping that.

"What about the second grade trip to the police station?" Hmm.

Robbers? Pickpockets? All-around bad guys? No, thanks.

First grade is the place for me.

On the zoo trip, I'll win the scavenger hunt because I already know where everything is!

It'll be fun to read those easy little
first grade books again!

And I'll definitely be the one
who's lost the most teeth.

Tyler's sisters say second grade is really hard.

And Mr. Glazer's class is hardest of all.

You have to learn the presidents by heart.

Forward AND backward.

Ready for the kind of spelling words he gives?

Platypus.

Rendezvous.

Discombobulated!

The only candy he allows on Halloween is black licorice.

(You probably need to know how to spell *licorice* too.)

On top of all that, you don't get to use the little kids' playground, the one with the twisty slide, during recess.

Tyler and I were pretty much kings of the twisty slide.

I wish everything could just stay the way it was.

At the park, Tyler's sisters call me over.

Probably to tell me more bad stuff about scary Mr. Glazer. But it doesn't matter,
because I'm not going to second grade.

"You know we were kidding, right?" Sabrina says.

"Yeah. Of course." I shrug one shoulder and make a *"Pfff"* sound.

Then I ask, "About what?"

Sabrina laughs. "About Mr. Glazer! He's kind of the best, actually."

"Really?" I ask.

"Better than Mrs. Herman?" Tyler asks.

"Well, only if you like basketball. He's all about basketball."

Hmm. I *do* like basketball . . .

"Sorry, Tyler. Nobody in Mrs. Herman's room is allowed to play basketball," Jacqueline says.

Sabrina shakes her head sadly.

Tyler looks back and forth between his sisters and then at me.

Tyler LOVES basketball.

"Maybe I could switch into Mr. Glazer's class," he says.

I know exactly how he feels.

So I remind him of the most important thing. "We'll see each other at recess every day!"

"No, you won't," Jacqueline says. "Mrs. Herman doesn't allow recess."

Wait a second.

That can't be true.

"Let me guess," I say.

I give Tyler a look.

The kings of the twisty slide cannot be tricked.

"She probably makes everyone memorize
the newspaper every day," I say.

"Who told you?" Jacqueline says.

"Even on weekends," Sabrina says.

I can almost see Tyler thinking.

Finally, he smiles and asks,

"So does that include all the ads?"

"Let's go," Jacqueline says. "These two little boogers have gotten too smart for us."

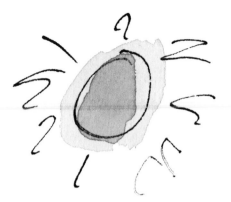

What does she expect?

That we're going to believe the crazy things she says?

It's not like we're in first grade anymore.